ABIYOYO RETURNS

By **Pete Seeger**

and **Paul DuBois Jacobs**

Illustrated by **Michael Hays**

Aladdin Paperbacks
New York   London   Toronto   Sydney

One day, a little girl played her drum as she marched around town.

Poom-i-ty, poom-poom, poom-i-ty, poom-poom.

Her father played the ukulele. Her mother played the flute. The three of them made up a family band. If there was a wedding or a birthday party, the little girl and her parents were always invited.

But their little town was in trouble. Over the years it had grown quickly. The valley that was once covered by forests was now bare. Every spring the town had floods. Every summer the town had droughts.

Something had to be done.

The townspeople put their heads together. "If we build a small dam," they said, "we could catch the spring rains and save the water for the fields in summer."

After careful planning, the town started to build the dam.
Everybody had to pitch in and *dig, dig, dig.*

But guess what happened?
They struck a boulder. It was bigger than it looked at first.

The townspeople thought they could dig around it.
But the more dirt they removed, the more rock they
uncovered.

The boulder was eNORmous!

They tried pulleys and levers and winches.
The boulder didn't budge. Work came to a halt.

Now, in this town they still told stories about the giants who lived in the old days. And one of these stories was about the giant Abiyoyo. They said he was as tall as a tree and could eat people up. But the little girl knew that long ago, her father and grandfather had saved the town by making Abiyoyo disappear.

"Papa," said the little girl, "I bet Abiyoyo could move that rock."
Her father laughed. "I suppose he could."
"Then why not bring him back?" she said. "Grandpa still has his magic wand. Once Abiyoyo moves the rock, *Zoop! Zoop!* Grandpa can make him disappear again."

"Bring back Abiyoyo?" said her mother. "The giant that eats people up?"

"We can make him lots of good food so he won't eat us," said the little girl.

"And if we run out of good things for him to eat?" asked her mother.

"Sing him lots of good songs!" said the little girl. "He won't get mad at us."

"Songs?" said her father. "That might not work this time."

"But if we don't bring back Abiyoyo," said the little girl, "we'll never get the dam built."

So that afternoon, the family went to see Grandpa.

"Bring back Abiyoyo?" Grandpa exclaimed. "A hungry giant is very dangerous."

"But no one else can move the rock," said the little girl.

"Perhaps you're right," said Grandpa. He opened his trunk of magic things and pulled out his wand. "Let's see if this dusty old thing still works."

And with a *Zoop!* the little girl's drum suddenly disappeared.
"Hey, Grandpa, give that back."
Zoop! The drum reappeared.
"I guess I still have the magic touch," Grandpa said with a giggle.

Over the next few days everybody in the town cooked
their best recipes and practiced their best songs.
Finally, they were ready.

Grandpa built a special fire out of special wood that made a special kind of smoke. Then he waved his wand and recited the magic words . . .

Zoooooop . . .

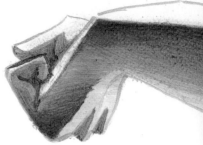

. . . *Zoooooop!*

There was Abiyoyo! Big as ever! Big as
a tall tree! With his long fingernails and his
slobbery teeth and his stinking feet.

Women screamed.

Eeekkk.

Strong men fainted.

Ohhh.

"Abiyoyo's returned!"

Abiyoyo yawned and stretched. **"OHHHH, I'M HUNGRY!"**

The townspeople brought out platters of spaghetti tofu chicken steak shrimp rice veggie fruit and all sorts of good things to eat.

Abiyoyo opened his mouth wide.

YEOWP! A whole spaghetti platter. Gone!

YUNK! A tray of strawberry shortcake.

Soon Abiyoyo had eaten everything.
"YUM!" The giant rubbed his tummy.
The little girl bravely walked up close.
"Abiyoyo, are you still strong?" she asked.

"OF COURSE!" roars Abiyoyo.

"Strong enough to lift that huge boulder?"

So Abiyoyo picks up the enormous boulder and throws it high in the air. Up it goes! One hundred feet!

Two hundred feet!

Down it comes!

KER-RUMPH!

"Hooray for Abiyoyo!"
People hug each other.
They dance.
Dogs bark for joy.

"I'M HUNGRY!" bellows Abiyoyo.
"But the food's all gone!"
Abiyoyo frowns.
The little girl grabs her drum.
Poom-i-ty poom-poom, poom-i-ty poom-poom.
Her father starts playing his ukulele.
Plink-i-ty plink-plink.
Her mother joins in on her flute.
Tootle-i-ty toot-toot.
Everybody begins to sing:

A - BI -YO - YO,   A - BI -YO - YO,   A - BI -YO - YO,   A - BI -YO - YO

The band plays faster.

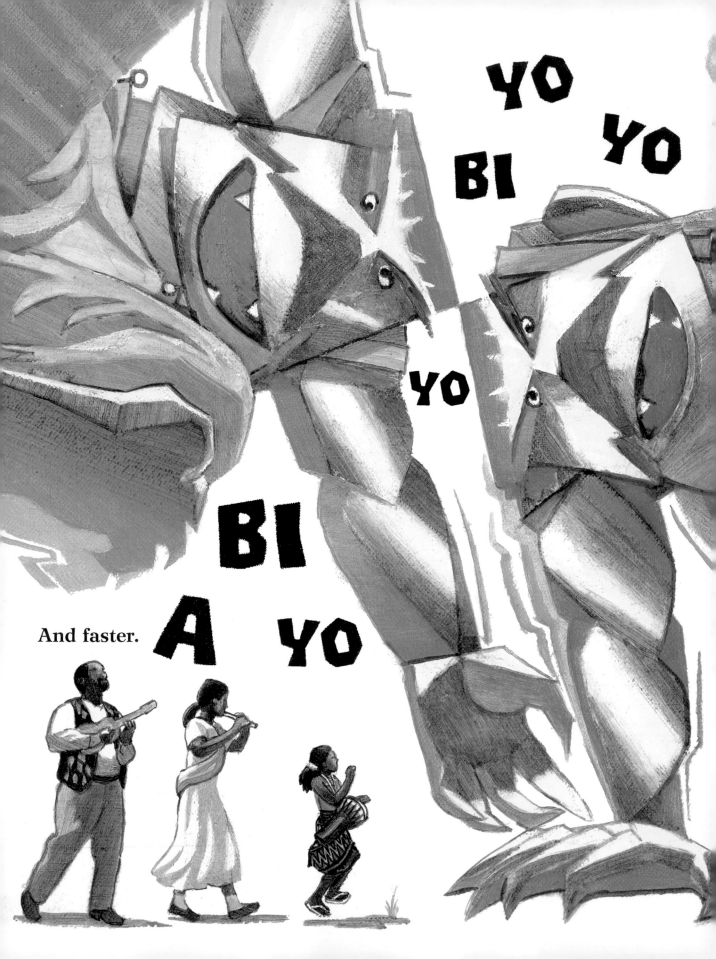

And faster.

He lay down and closed his eyes. Soon he was snoring.

"Now's our chance!" whispered the little girl. "But where's Grandpa with his magic wand?"

"He was right over there." Her mother pointed.

"Oh, no!" cried the little girl. "Grandpa, are you all right?"
"I'm okay," said Grandpa. "The boulder just missed me."
"But where's your magic wand?" the little girl whispered.
"I'm not sure," he said.

"Here it is," said the little girl's father.

Everybody looked. First at the broken wand. Then at the snoring giant. Then at the little girl.

"You got us into this," the townspeople said. "Now, get us out."

"There's only one thing to do," said the little girl. "Let's make Abiyoyo lots of good food, then he won't want to eat us. And if we sing him lots of good songs, he won't get mad at us."

ZZZZ

So in time the little town learned to live with its giant. Abiyoyo slept in the barn with his head sticking out one side and his feet sticking out the other. He even learned to brush his slobbery teeth.

And he got so fond of the little girl and her parents, they became like a family. They even helped him wash his stinking feet.

And the townspeople?

Well, with Abiyoyo's help, they built their small dam. Most important, they never forgot the need to share good food, and they never forgot how to share good songs.

And the last anyone saw, Abiyoyo was happily planting new trees.

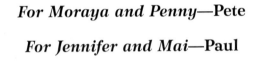

For Moraya and Penny—Pete

For Jennifer and Mai—Paul

For Becky—Michael

First Aladdin Paperbacks edition November 2004

Text copyright © 2001 by Sanga Music, Inc.
Illustrations copyright © 2001 by Michael Hays

ALADDIN PAPERBACKS
An imprint of Simon & Schuster
Children's Publishing Division
1230 Avenue of the Americas
New York, NY 10020

Also available in a Simon & Schuster Books for Young Readers hardcover edition.
Designed by Michael Hays
The text of this book was set in 14-point Wilke Bold.

Manufactured in China
10 9

The Library of Congress has cataloged the hardcover edition as follows:
Seeger, Pete. 1919-
Abiyoyo returns/ by Pete Seeger and Paul DuBois Jacobs; illustrated by Michael Hays.
p.   cm.
Summary: Based on a South African tale, this story tells what happens when a giant who had been banished from a town by a magician
thirty years earlier is called back to save the town from flooding.
ISBN 978-0-689-83271-0 (hc.)
[1. Folklore—South Africa. 2. Magicians—Folklore. 3. Giants—Folklore.]
I. Jacobs, Paul DuBois. II. Hays, Michael, 1956-ill. III. Title.
PZ8.1.S453 Ae 2001
398.2'0968'01—dc21
00-045066
ISBN-13: 978-0-689-87054-5 ISBN-10: 0-689-87054-X (Aladdin pbk.)

0816 SCP